W9-BEV-990

Does this book **belong** to **you** 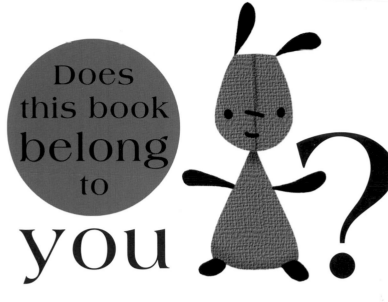?

Yup!

Then you can write your name **here:**

....

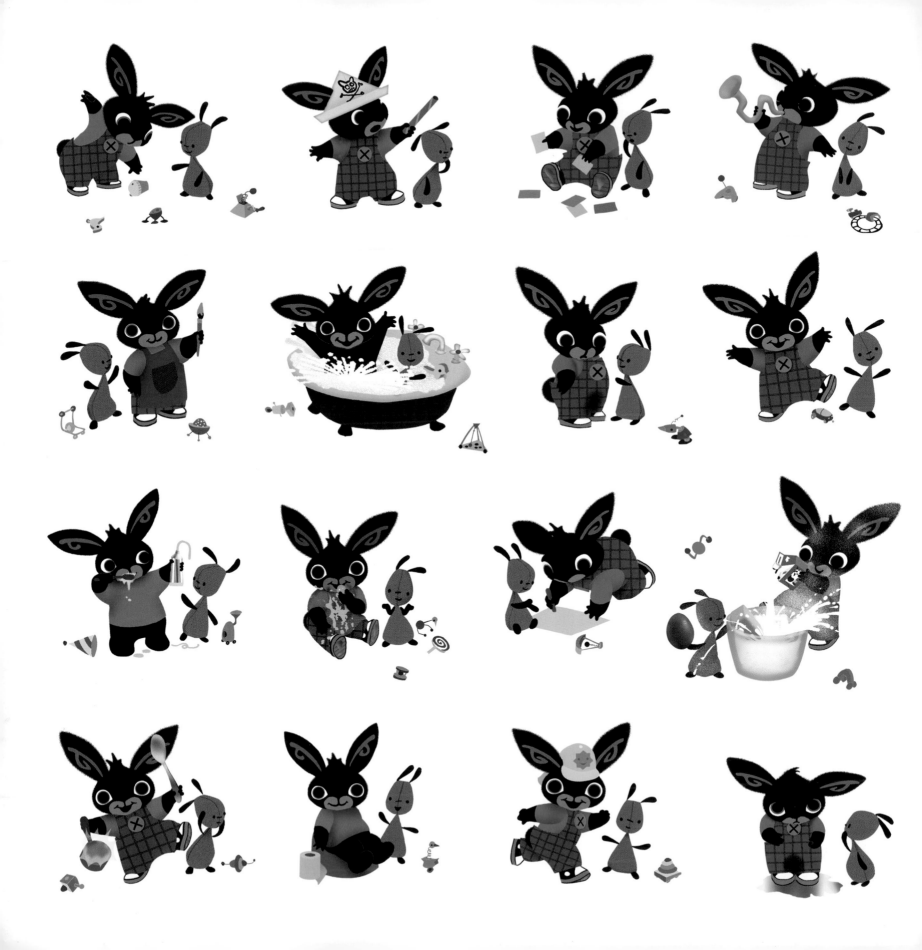

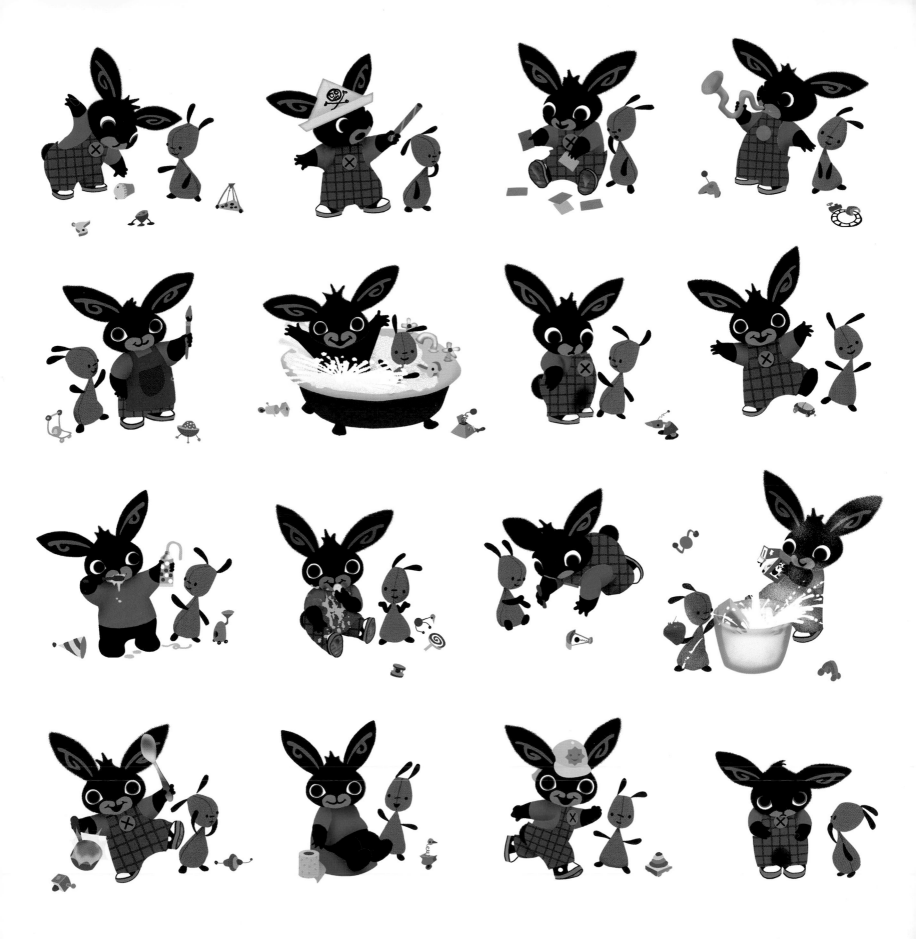

Ready to Read?

Bing
by Ted Dewan

Get Dressed

Yup!

Bing

Get Dressed

by
Ted Dewan

HarperCollins *Children's Books*

**Round the corner,
Not far away,
Bing begins another day.**

Wake up
Bing.

Wake
up
Flop.

Let's
get

dressed.

OK now,
let's
take off
those

pyjamas.

can **YOU**
put your
shirt
on

all by
yourself?

Yup!

Good for you Bing Bunny.

Hey, can you put your **pants** on all by **yourself?**

Hey, can you put your socks on

all by yourself?

Yup!

Good for you
Bing Bunny.

Hey,
can you put your
shoes
on

all by yourself?

Yup!

Hey Bing!

Wait a minute!

Dungarees!

You forgot your dungarees!

!

What do we do now?

The dungarees won't fit
over your shoes.

You'll
have to
take your shoes off.

NOW
you can
put on your
dungarees

and **NOW** your shoes.

Good for you
Bing Bunny.

Now you're all ready.

Oops.

What's up Bing?

Oh dear. Poor Bing.

Looks like we've had an accident.

Don't worry Bing.

It's no big thing.

We'll just get dressed